AND THE WALTZ OF COLOURS

BASIL
AND THE
WALTZ OF COLOURS

CRINA-LUDMILA CRISTEA

Illustrated by **BENJA HUGHES**

© Copyright

All rights reserved. No part of this publication may be reproduced, distributed, or transmitted in any form or by any means, including photocopying, recording, or other electronic or mechanical methods, without the prior written permission of the publisher, except in the case of brief quotations embodied in critical reviews and certain other non-commercial uses permitted by copyright law. For permission requests, write to the publisher, addressed "Attention: Permission request BASIL" at the email below.

crinalcristea@gmail.com

For more stories, follow the artists on Instagram:

@lilybloomwriter and @benjayoungfox

Illustrations: © Benja Hughes, 2021

Story, Interior, and Cover Design:

© Crina-Ludmila Cristea, 2021

First Edition Published Independently in 2021

This British Edition Published Independently in 2022

For the strong and gentle,

and for everyone else, too.

Especially for you.

Hello Dear Friend,

Please snuggle up tight and relax.

I'm going to tell you a story long forgotten, about the early days when my 14th great-grandfather was just a young child, often guarding sheep in the fields with his dog and sometimes his cat. Back then, the old oaks, the wonderful chestnuts, and the large fruit trees growing now in our orchard weren't even seeds.

Yes, that was very, very, *very* long ago *indeed*.

This grand city was only a small village, situated at the foot of a mountain shrouded in mist and mystery. The light or, rather, the shadows cast by the mountain on the village were… strange, to say the least. The path to the mountain was often treacherous and not many villagers took it. Especially not after the sun went down and darkness fell.

But late one night, after a long, hard day of work,

and after having a little too much grape juice at a party and losing a bet to his best friend Akiva, Sean Basil stumbled on that very path. He was supposed to collect water from a spring deep in the mountain, give it to his friends as proof of honoring the bet he'd lost, and then head back home to blissful sleep.

"It was not meant to be," some would say. "It was fate," others would add.

Whatever it was, Sean Basil did not make it back to his friends that night.

In the early hours of the morning, after the strenuous walk to the spring, Sean Basil was joyously returning to the village with a full bottle of icy water. He had walked a mile or so on the twisted moonlit pathway, sometimes singing — *and rather loudly for that hour* — when he took a wrong turn, slipped, and fell. He rolled down the hill for quite some time and then stopped just short of hitting his head on a boulder. Eyes wide open, Basil massaged his injured shoulder and grimaced as stinging pain shot through his muscles. He brushed the leaves and the broken, decaying sticks away from his clothes, checked his satchel containing the water bottle — it was intact — and considered himself lucky. He could have been dead.

But all of a sudden, he found himself lifted high into the air by something very large and strong. The moon shone on the creature's claws. They were long and sharp — *like deadly blades*. Everything happened *so* fast. With breathtaking, graceful precision, the creature gently but swiftly moved Basil from her claws onto her back, and carried him away. Basil held on for dear life.

As he stared up and down with eyes bulging, his body frozen and terrified, Basil began to understand what had just happened. A gang of nightmarish creatures, each of them twice as big as him, with bared teeth and saliva dripping from their hungry jaws, had been near the boulder, ready to devour him. He had narrowly escaped from accidentally cracking his head on the boulder, but, one more step and he would have been eaten alive. Without the aid of the bizarre creature, his story would have ended right then and there. But she saved him. It was the strangest and most curious thing which had ever happened to Basil in his entire life so far, and that led to a series of unexpected events.

For a moment, Basil thought he had fallen from the lake into the well, as the old saying goes, but then the creature turned, gazed at him, and asked him where his home was. Astonished that the dragon — *for that was what the creature appeared to be* — could speak, Basil found himself explaining exactly where he lived with his wife and children, his 101-year-old grandma, a cat, a dog, and a couple of sheep. Basil wondered to himself why he revealed *that* much. He certainly had no intention of ever putting his small, precious family in danger. It then occurred to him that he spoke as if hypnotized. He panicked inside even more, but he kept his calm.

"My wife is a master of martial arts, and my grandma is still the sharpest and greatest detective of her time. The two of them and my children are expecting me to get home safely. If something happens and I don't arrive home in a good manner, they will find you," Basil added, just in case the dragon was planning to feast on him.

The dragon smiled, slowed her flight, and landed as gently as she could on a field behind Basil's home.

"Next time, don't stay out so late. There is danger in the shadows."

The dragon winked at Basil and took flight, leaving the shocked man holding his bottle with icy water safely to his chest.

Other than his family, nobody believed Basil when he told them what had happened. In fact, once he claimed he had flown perched atop a dragon he named YELLOW, everyone made fun of him and called him 'Basil the Brave'. People thought the whole idea was just too ridiculous to take seriously. Unwittingly, though, they were right to call him Basil the Brave. As later events would show, he was a very brave individual indeed.

Basil had flown atop a dragon. And he named it 'Yellow' because, unlike anything he had seen before, the creature wasn't black and white. It looked entirely different from anything else he had ever experienced and it made his heart flutter with joy.

But because the dragon had set him down gently and surreptitiously flown away, how could anyone believe him? He had no proof. On top of that, the world Basil lived in back then was made entirely of black and white, or shades of. Fields, rivers, the sky, the sun, the houses, the people — *everything* was colourless! Nobody had seen or heard of such a thing as Yellow, like Basil tried to describe. Fed up with the sarcastic comments, Basil decided to go in search of proof so that his people would believe him. He couldn't quite explain what he had seen, but he knew that it was real. He didn't know how it was possible or what was really going on, but he wasn't a liar, and he planned to uncover the enigma.

"I'll show them," he muttered.

He prepared the essentials for his journey and spent his last hours of the night trying to get some rest. His best friend Akiva was supposed to join him, but in the early morning of Basil's departure, he had another family emergency, more pressing than Basil's. Akiva decided to remain at home and take care of Stephan Valentin Forrest, his middle child, who was bitten by a bug angel. The child was out of serious danger for the time being, but he required the care of his father. There was nothing others could do for the child. It was the time of shaping and strengthening the bond for Akiva and his son, so Basil ventured to go on his own, unwilling to ask his best friend — *his brother*, not by blood, but by *choice* — to leave his child alone at a time like that, or delay his exploration any longer.

Basil said his well wishes to Akiva and his son, fed the sheep, as usual, patted his cat and dog, hugged his children and grandma, kissed his wife, and then went on in search of Yellow, leaving almost everything and everyone he knew behind. He carried with him just a few things for protection and aid in case of emergency.

Basil walked for hours on the country road, and then set off through the forest, in search of the dragon. After a while, he came across a secluded clearing, with a field full of plump cabbage and white clover. Basil sat down to rest and *that* was the moment when he noticed it. There was something *odd* about one of those clovers. It had four leaves instead of three, which was already unusual enough, but, much stranger than that, the clover was unlike the usual black and white clovers which Basil had seen all his life in the fields.

"It's hard to explain," he said to himself, "but somehow this four-leaf clover is *bright*, and *popping* from the rest, just like the dragon, yet in a distinct and very different way. The dragon — Yellow — felt *warm* and *calm*. This feels more... *fresh*." Basil carefully wrote the observations in his notebook.

He cradled the clover between his fingers, and was about to pick it as proof of his discovery. But right in that very moment, the delicate clover started to yell and cry as if all hell had broken loose!

As soon as Basil had retreated, quite startled, the clover stopped crying. Basil's intention wasn't to hurt it, so he let it be, but, at the same time, Basil was also intrigued by hearing a clover that could yell. *This* four-leaf clover wasn't something he saw every day — it was *extra* special. Basil named the clover GREEN and in the very moment that he said the word, Basil thought he noticed a smile on its face. But perhaps he imagined it. Although he was disappointed he couldn't take the clover to convince the people back home that there was something very strange going on, Basil journeyed on, still ecstatic thanks to his marvelous discovery. He even started singing out loud again, that's how excited he was.

As he walked and walked some more, Basil came upon a field full of cornflowers and he stopped to enjoy the view. In the middle of the field, however, he discovered there was one cornflower that stood out from the rest of the black and white ones Basil was accustomed to. This was peculiar and curious to Basil, but this strangeness made him *happy* somehow. He named this cornflower BLUE. He considered picking her as a lovely gift for his wife, and as proof to the villagers, since she was so gorgeous and surely one of a kind. But Blue started yelling, too, just as Green had. He realized that picking her would be disrespectful and harmful. Since he was someone who always tried to heal rather than hurt, Basil took a wistful glance at Blue and then carried on with his journey.

"I'll find something else to give as proof to my people, and I'll think of another gift for my beloved Sasha," he said.

Again, he strode out along the path, and soon he came upon a field full of pumpkins. In the middle of the field, there was one pumpkin bigger than all the rest. But the greatest and most impressive thing about this pumpkin was not its spectacular size, but the fact that it was most definitely not black and white. It was not at all like any of the other pumpkins. Basil called this particular pumpkin ORANGE because, after the long and tiring walk, the sight of this one gave him *a boost of energy*. He considered taking Orange with him since it looked sturdy and well resilient for the journey ahead, but the pumpkin was just too large.

By then, Basil had begun to realize that his world was changing. It was as if each beat and brush of the wind brought new substance into it, and he embraced the transformation, more focused on his discoveries now than on proving others wrong. The more he searched, the more differences he found; the more delight he felt, the more questions he had. He looked at *everything* in a new way. He had an epiphany, as some would say.

Thick leaves crunching under his feet, Basil advanced through the ancient forest. The more he walked, the deeper and darker the forest became. Eventually, though, amid all that darkness, Basil discovered a place lit by the sun as if it had been poured with gold. Exhausted but elated, he dropped to his knees at the luminous spot, which revealed a spring, from which he drank plenty of fresh water to quench his thirst. The moss around the spring was soft under his palms and it reminded Basil of his beloved wife and children. He smiled as he touched his chest with his left palm and rubbed the spot gently. No matter where he went, they were in his heart, guiding his way and lighting his path. No matter how far from home he was, or how difficult the journey, he believed he would see and hug them again *before the end of all ends*.

Basil marveled at the waterfalls of flowers hanging from trees and the thick roots covering the earth, going deeper than one could see — communicating with the underground world. He decided to stay a while by the spring, and munched on a leaf of wild garlic as he wandered around, stretching his feet. He whistled a song he learned many moons ago, when he himself was a young boy, and picked fresh stinging nettles to cook for a hearty soup.

Basil stopped after a while and observed a young mulberry growing under an old chestnut, mischievously weaving its way through the canopy towards the sky. Hazelnuts were plentiful around, and an elder wasn't far off. Basil sensed it. He knew its berries are good for colds, if cooked well, otherwise they're poisonous, and its flowers smell heady and wonderful; the stems are hollow — good to blow and make fire.

Basil also collected a few twigs and leaves from a tree he didn't know, and picked a bunch of seeds which had fallen on the ground beneath. He figured they could be useful to study and plant, once his search for the dragon was over.

He approached the spring and drank from it once again. The warm sun shone on Basil's back. Trickles of sweat went down the sides of his face, water dripping from his beard. He splashed and cleaned himself a little. As he wiped his face and lifted his gaze from the clear, shimmering water, he spotted a deer staring at him. The animal ran away, scared, shortly after, and Basil wondered why. As he took a bite from a hunk of bread baked by his wife, he smiled at the shape she had carved into it — a tree. Emerging from his daydream, Basil suddenly noticed something else through the ancient, twisted branches: three little dragons. By Basil's quick calculations, they weren't really so small but as big as him, if not slightly bigger. The dragons, too, were standing out from the black and white, *popping* in front of Basil's astonished eyes. Basil held his breath momentarily, stunned by the vibrant beauty and cuteness revealed to him. They were *so* eye-catching.

He noticed the little dragons seemed a bit confused, and one of them even appeared scared.

"I've told you we shouldn't have gone behind Mama's back. Now we're lost in this dark, frightful forest."

"Are you alright?" asked Basil suddenly

The three small dragons tracked the source of the voice, and when they found it, they instantly fixed their gaze on Basil. They were a bit wary to talk to him at first, but as they sniffed the air coming from his direction and assessed the situation, they decided it was safe to approach and speak with Basil.

"We're lost, Mister Human. Mama told us not to play in here without her, but… um… we did, and got ourselves into trouble. Now we can't find our way back."

"Maybe I can help you. Could you tell me what your home looks like and how the sun shines on it, if at all?"

The smallest dragon, who also seemed to be the bravest, started to answer again.

But all at once, towering behind the three baby dragons, appeared twelve nasty creatures, the same ones that had been planning to feast on Basil the night Yellow had saved his life.

Basil quickly positioned himself in the path of the creatures and called the dragons behind him. Even if the dragons were as big as him, Basil could tell they were only young — perhaps about the same age as his own children. He was ready to protect them with his own life. And even though they had only just met Basil, the dragons instinctively trusted him and did as they were told. The danger was too great to do anything else.

"Stay behind me," he repeated, and then raised his carved stick, bravely facing the terrifying creatures. With his mind's eye, Basil briefly saw his best friend Akiva, who was valiant and strong, too — he would have been a great help in that moment. In fact, even though Akiva wasn't there physically, Basil felt he was present in spirit. Basil stood rooted to the spot, channelling and gathering his energy, and trying his best not to lose it. There were *babies* depending on him. He could have run, of course, since all of them were in mortal danger. Most would have understood that choice, but the thought didn't even cross Basil's mind. If it did, it sure didn't take over his mind and body, which is still quite remarkable. Instead, Basil gently furrowed his brow, carefully watched and quickly appraised the frightening beasts.

They moved as a pack this time, and were advancing to attack and make a meal of Basil and the baby dragons.

Basil dreaded the very idea of using force against another being. He always found another way. But time was of the essence and in the face of such peril, he steeled himself for the fight. Beads of sweat started to form on Basil's forehead. He kept his arms and legs wide, making himself appear as large as he could in front of the beasts, protecting the baby dragons from the imminent, life-threatening attack. The head of the beast pack sneered and shrieked with a glow in its eyes that delivered the conspicuous message: "You're my lunch and you're not getting away from us this time".

A great shadow passed overhead then, and the air itself seemed to quake. In the blink of an eye, and to Basil's profound relief, Yellow had arrived, just in time. She landed heavily, shaking the earth under her body, and released the most blood-curdling shriek Basil had ever heard in his entire life. During the few moments when he and the snarling creatures were stunned and deafened, Yellow gently enfolded the small dragons with her massive wings.

"Here you were, my little hearts," she said calmly. "I've told you not to wander in here without me. This forest is full of all sorts of dangerous and nefarious creatures. There's trouble right now, isn't there?"

The little dragons nodded.

Perfectly composed, Yellow turned and addressed the clamouring creatures, gazing deeply into their eyes:

"Why don't you go pick your own nettles, eh?"

Confused, the twelve creatures glanced at one another.

Meanwhile, back in the village and unbeknownst to Basil, as he discovered and named Green and Blue and so on, on his journey, the people began to see changes all around them, bit by bit, with each passing day.

At first, the villagers were terrified, running and screaming, unable to understand what was going on and pondering what kind of peril or illness might have taken over their world. And they hadn't heard from Basil in a very long time. They thought he was probably lost, or trapped somewhere, or even *entirely gone* — *perished* from their world. They thought *the worst* happened to him. The villagers felt sorry they had made fun of Basil, and fondly remembered the many great times they spent with him instead. Many cried, ran, and hid in despair, not knowing what to do. They thought they were probably going to perish pretty soon, too. Akiva tried to convince the villagers that Basil was capable of handling many situations, even deadly ones, and that things couldn't be as bad as they seemed to some. However, they found that hard to believe with the chaotic scenes constantly happening all around them.

But one bright morning, the lookout reported seeing a strong figure coming up on the dusty road. Akiva's face brightened, and he smiled a big smile.

"Welcome back, brother! It's been a while. I wish I could have been there with you," said Akiva.

"You were, brother," said Basil mysteriously, smiling and embracing him.

So Basil came back, well and safe, and the people were a bit more relieved.

Basil observed the village he had left behind months ago. Many of the things and the people he used to know were now colourised, no longer plain black and white. Basil took a closer look. The fields he worked on were mostly green. Under his feet and as far as his eyes could see, dandelions made thick, gentle and tickling carpets — stable lakes of yellow and green. The trees from which many birds chirped and flew were budding with yellow blooms and fresh green leaves. The bees were buzzing and the butterflies were dancing — they were all brushing their bottoms on wildflowers and even breaking wind from time to time, just like humans do. Those were some strange, funny, and smelly moments indeed, like a marvellous dream turned into reality. A few of Basil's friends had bright blue eyes, just like he did, although his eyes seemed to change with the weather or the shift of light and looked green or hazel sometimes. Many people, among whom was his best friend Akiva, had dark hair and dark eyes. Others had yellow hair, green eyes, and rosy cheeks. They all looked one of a kind. Basil noticed only a few bits and pieces remained plain black and white. That made him happy because he knew what it meant.

"For you and your people, more changes will be coming," he remembered Yellow saying to him. "I know it here and here that *you* are ready," she continued, pointing to her immense belly, where Basil presumed her heart was, and to her head. "But they might not be. Some will be scared out of their minds. They will need your help."

"I understand. I will do my best," Basil had promised, nodding slowly and thoughtfully. He bowed to Yellow, hugged the little dragons who rushed to him, and then he left their supremely large yet cosy nest.

The colour of the world was being passed on to him, and to others, slowly but surely. Basil *cherished* the gift he'd been given. He revelled in it and realized his simple yet adventurous search for the dragon led to witnessing and participating in the incredible experience — he suspected many more to come.

But Basil also found frightened villagers who would not leave their homes, afraid of the change, just as Yellow said.

You may wonder why many of the villagers reacted like that despite the gift of such beauty.

When people are used to the way things are, sometimes they find it hard to adjust to something new, even if it is exquisite and may further enrich their lives. They might see it as a threat instead of a blessing, unless someone gives them a reason to look at things from a new perspective.

With the trust and help of his best friend Akiva, Basil brought the people together and helped them understand the *new* world they were living in, which was not new really — it had always been there before, they just could not see it for what it actually was. When one took a chance and explored it — *as Basil did* — that decision created a chain reaction which led to more being seen. It inspired others.

Soon, the villagers understood how things worked, more or less. Even the most sceptical of them came to terms with the changes and embraced the phenomenon which was named THE COLOURS. They had yet to see the famous Yellow dragon Basil told them about, but they didn't have to wait much longer for that.

News about The Colours spread across the entire world soon, and a large party followed at which Basil the Brave was the guest of honour.

He arrived with his entire family — yes, *even* his sheep, his dog, his cat, and *especially* his athletic grandma, who had recently turned 102 years old and was super-excited about the party. They were all bundled up and perched on the magnificent dragon renamed YELLOW FLAME since plenty of other yellow beings and things appeared each day.

Yellow Flame surpassed her reputation as she flew across the sky and spread her majestic wings wide for everyone to finally see her colourful flight in all its strength and beauty. With a flourish and a rush of air, she landed them safely on the ground.

The three small dragons — VIOLET, INDIGO, and RED — followed and landed, somewhat safely, too. They were still learning.

People cheered and greeted all of them. They were not afraid since Basil had announced to them in advance that these were friendly dragons.

Beautiful dancers, dressed in dazzling colours, braced the evening air full of vitality and mesmerized the audience with their movements. Everything was *so* ethereal. It was the quintessence of a happy time. Basil the Brave glanced around at everyone to make sure he wasn't drunk or dreaming, and that they, too, were seeing and hearing what he was witnessing.

All was pristine and infused with the beauty of The Colours. The food was appealing and tasted delicious, the scent of flowers was comforting and wonderful, the music… oh, the music was ineffable, and *everyone* was hugging. Life was simply better than ever before.

Even the nasty creatures were invited to the ravishingly beautiful event. Yellow and Basil had spoken with them and found out they were famished and hadn't managed to provide suitable food for their babies in months. When they closed in on Basil and the three young dragons, they were really desperate. The creatures agreed they should have behaved differently, especially since dragons or humans weren't appropriate food to sustain their kind. They sincerely apologized and promised not to behave badly again. With things cleared and out of the way, they were welcomed to join the celebration. Their reception was a bit cold at first, but everyone warmed up to them eventually, as that was the way — to talk with one another and listen, to forgive, and to party. To have faith in the goodness of others. It didn't hurt that the creatures were great singers, too, unafraid to show their wonky dancing steps.

Three ladies, newly arrived at the celebration and who looked charming and strangely reminiscent of Green, Blue, and Orange — the beings Basil had met on his journey — glanced, winked, and smiled at him. Basil stared for a moment, bewildered, then grinned and winked back. He approached the ladies and respectfully bowed in front of them.

"How strange and fascinating nature is," Basil said softly, almost lost for words.

"Wait to see RAINBOW dancing in the sky," whispered the elegant lady with piercing blue eyes and dulcet voice, teasing him.

"Who's that?" asked Basil, always curious and wanting to know more.

"Just you wait. It will happen tomorrow at lunchtime, after the rain shower. It will be *quite* the spectacle," added the poised lady with fascinating green eyes.

"We're going to give you all the show of a lifetime, really. It will be the biggest RAINBOW ever, and then smaller ones will follow, from time to time, here and there, forever," continued the lady with striking orange hair, clearly delighted.

Basil raised his eyebrows, a plethora of questions running around in his head, then smiled, bowed again, kissed the ladies' hands, and invited them over. He introduced them to his wife, his best friend Akiva, and the rest of their family.

They partied late into the night and continued for weeks, as was the custom in those days. It was much later when they started to set shorter parties, and that rule lasted for quite some time, but that's a different story and I'll tell it to you another time.

When asked, Basil the Brave told everyone at the party how he first encountered Yellow Flame and the others, and the audience burst into a volley of laughter at the spirited tale. This time, however, everyone believed him. His nickname had stuck — it stuck for the right reasons. After all, it is no small thing flying with a dragon, facing doubts and beasts, and making life-changing decisions such as exploring the unknown and bringing colour to the world.

To Be Continued...

BEHIND THE SCENES

HOW DID WE MAKE THIS BOOK?

Author's Note

There are many things that must come together for someone to complete a book and make it available. I will mention them here briefly, in an attempt to raise awareness of the creativity and effort that go on when making a book, especially as an indie author, and also because when I was younger, discovering books and stories, I was curious and interested in how they were made. I still am, and maybe you are, too.

First things first.
I started writing this story at the very end of March 2021, at a round glass table, in the open-plan kitchen of the flat I've been living in since November 2018. Bits and pieces were written step by step, sometimes to the cheerful music of a train going past, other times to the chirping of birds, people, and cars. Once construction noise was added to that, it all turned into a real interesting sound mix.

The written story — initially titled THE COLOURS, then *The Dance of Colours* — was more or less done a couple of weeks later. I was not working on it every day, every hour — *just to be clear*. I shared it with a couple of trustworthy readers — we writers call those *beta readers* — and I received a lot of useful feedback that helped me improve it.

I have debated on the title for quite some time. I wanted it to be easy to remember and also not likely to have been, or to be, used by another writer. I eventually settled on the current one because I felt it sounded elegant and suitable for the overall story. *Waltz* is not the easiest word for some, but I felt it was a nice challenge. While evoking a time passed, the title also mentioned the protagonist. I considered people would be drawn to that because it felt like an invitation to find out about someone's life — sort of a call to action to embark on an adventure.

Although I anticipated to be finished with the project by the end of October and have it printed and published soon after, the final touches to the book were made in December 2021. Some things are worth waiting for — *hey, I'm an author showing off my baby, what can I say? The labour took some time, but now the baby is finally here. I don't expect to be quiet about it anytime soon, as most parents wouldn't.*

While putting this book together, I developed a 'small' addiction to sweet roasted chestnuts — *one of the delights of autumn* — which kept me nourished and inspired. I gazed from time to time at the Manchester skyline, painted with emerging new buildings and beautiful sunsets sneaking through a couple of leafy treetops, *rain or sunshine, most of the year*, or with snowflakes gently falling at the end of November, while I was still pondering over certain words and matters. Although I consider myself a countryside person at heart, I can see the appeal and hypnotic gaze of the city at night when its many buildings are lit, often well into the morning, and I did wonder, once or twice, what Basil and Yellow Flame would make of all of this.

I initially thought, because many of the illustrations were going to be black and white, or shades of, that it will take less time to illustrate them. The black ink needed several coats and time to dry, however, and that made the process take longer than anticipated. Benja was also working and releasing his music videos in those months, and I was working on writing and designing other books, too. It worked fine because it gave us more time to notice things since we weren't able to move faster. It allowed us to pay more attention to details, and taught me to be more patient. The manuscript went through many more edits thanks to these kinds of challenges, and I think it was for the best.

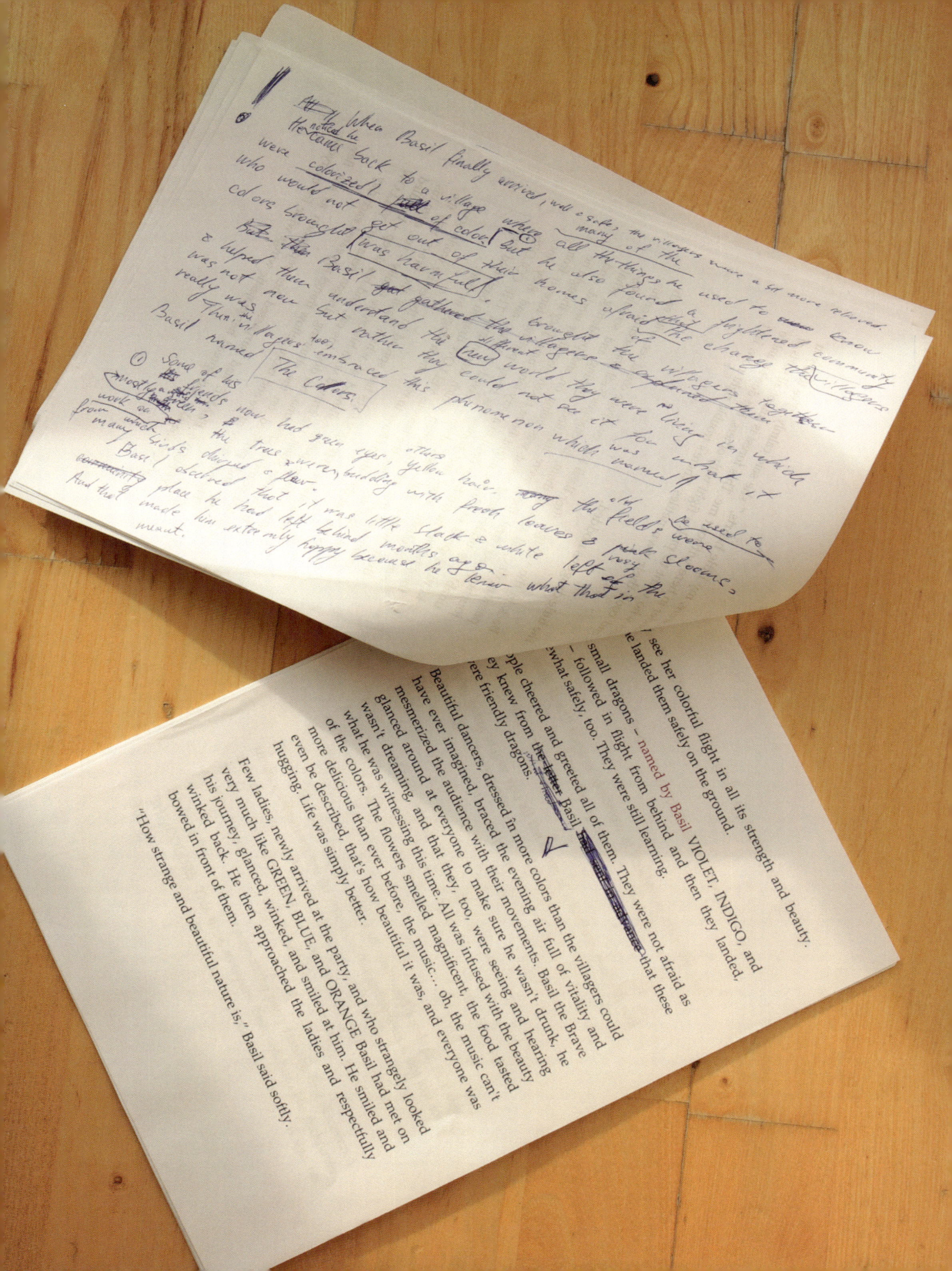

The evolution of the cover

Early on, I had a strong idea of how I wanted the cover to look. I knew the book was going to be a hardcover format, 8.25x11 inches in size, so this is the initial design I did for it, before the illustrations and the story edits were completed. I used an image from my other book illustrated by Benja — *Miss Camelia and the Hugelkultur Mound*.

I did that because it helps me to have a visual representation of the project I'm working on. It makes it feel more real and that is helpful when I am going through difficult moments. Writing a book can be isolating at times, more often than not. I actually do not mind it, I like being surrounded by books and stories, but it can be overwhelming sometimes. It may so happen that the world is 'burning' and some writers — *many, in fact* — are more preoccupied with the state of our stories rather than with what is going on in the outside world. That can be alienating for people. It helps to acknowledge that circumstances change, while books and stories can last forever, or, at least, for a very long time — they're like perennial plants. Putting a lot of time and attention into them is understandable, I think, rather than excessively consuming energy on things that one has no control over.

I didn't know exactly what was going to be the cover illustration, but after putting together a list of scenes for Benja, I knew I wanted it to be either a close-up with Basil staring into the eyes of Yellow Flame, or a medium scene with Basil and Yellow Flame in full view, so we could see how impressive the dragon is and at the same time encapsulate what the story is about.

Months later, after the illustrations were in the making and most of the text edits were done on my side, I started focusing on the cover again. Benja had done an early sketch of the dragon to help us figure out how Yellow Flame will look like alongside Basil, especially in terms of scale and colour, for the entire book, and long ago I decided I wanted black, white, and yellow on the cover. I wasn't sure if I wanted blue on it or not. After doing some mock-ups on my phone, I realized the black,

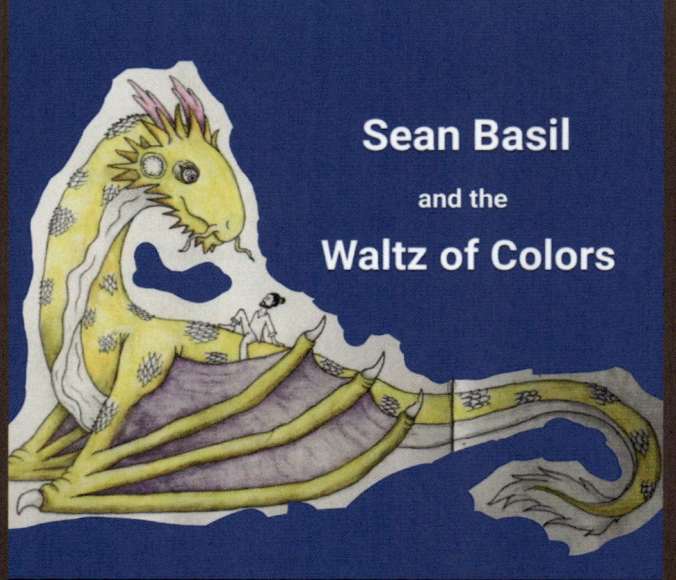

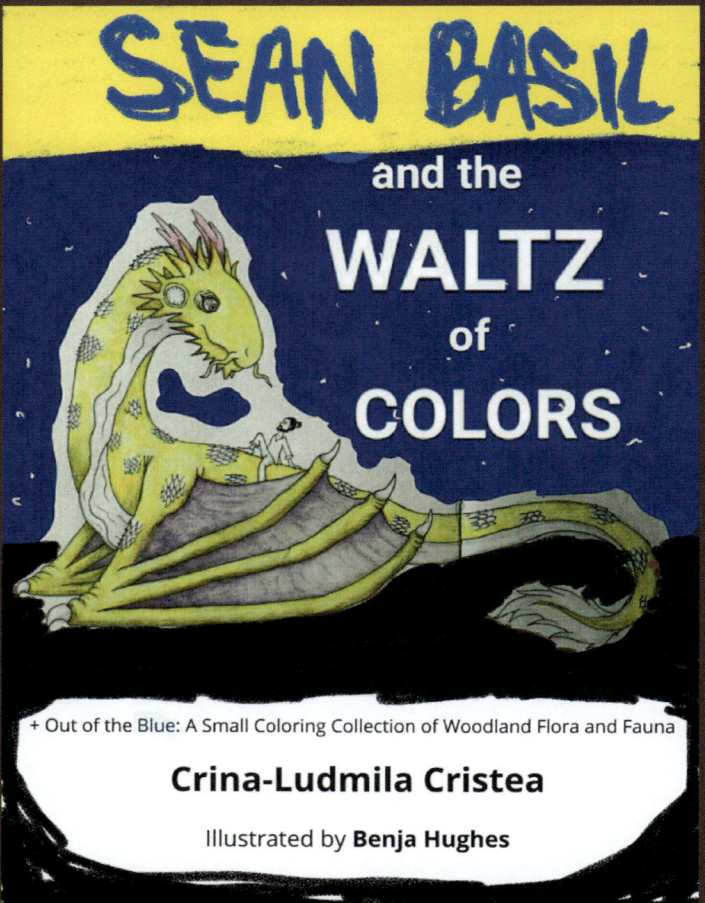

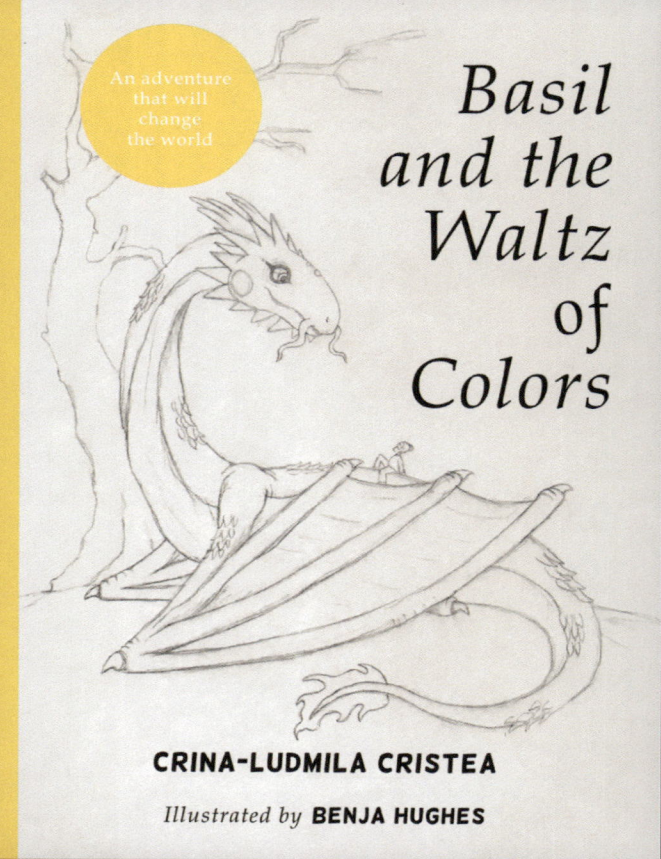

yellow, and white combo looked too stark for my liking, so I decided I wanted (dark) blue, too. In my mind, it stood for the time — the night and the sky — the mystery, and for Basil's eye colour (although that was a different shade of blue, but still). Benja agreed and said he liked the idea of the blue being kind of an extension of Basil's eye colour. It made sense.

I wasn't satisfied with the placement of the title and the author names, however — *not for this kind of book anyway* — and, after a while, I arrived at another design which felt somewhat more pleasing. Eventually, after Benja saw many of these designs, and read my notes and ideas, he created the final illustration. Then, after I tried combinations of fonts, sizes, and colours I thought appropriate for the feel and look of the story, I finished the design on my laptop.

There is a lot of time and research that goes into making a book cover. There are many unseen details that add up and help the final design to be as it is in the end. It involves scrolling through many (Instagram) photos of book covers, or going to libraries and bookshops to browse and look at books. During the making of this book, both Benja and I researched and took inspiration from dozens (and probably hundreds) of images, and experimented with illustrating the story and the scenes from many points of view. They would occupy too much space to share them all here. I hope this gives you at least an idea — *a flavour* — of the process.

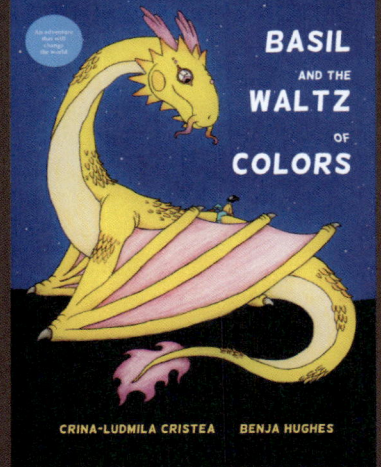

How the interior illustrations were created

I mentioned that I made a list of scenes for the story so Benja knew what was needed and how I wanted each paramount moment to be illustrated. There were sixteen main scenes (including the cover). Some of them were detailed but straightforward (with one point-of-view option), while others had more suggested (sometimes two or three).

Benja did a mock-up storyboard for most of the scenes and we exchanged notes and ideas on what was great, what needed to be added, taken away, or depicted in a slightly different way. He didn't draw all fifteen interior scenes, but he drew most of them and that was very helpful.

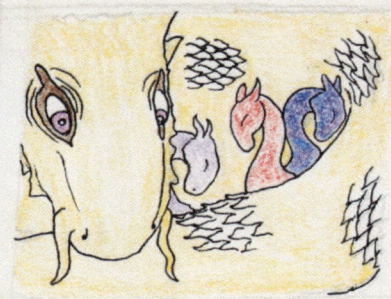

He then proceeded to create the actual large illustrations for the story. Bit by bit, he drew them by pencil, then added ink and colour to them. Some things changed during this process and the scenes were similar to the storyboard, but greatly improved. I believe the process of drawing a storyboard first and only afterwards creating the final illustrations is a time-consuming, but worthwhile, process. It enriches the main story. It helped us avoid and realize some of the mistakes made before putting them in the book.

In these images you can see some of the sketches Benja made early on, how they evolved over the course of several months, and, if you've read the book up to this point, you now know how these scenes turned out in the end.

After a while, I realized Basil needed a friend. He was written as a friendly character — *in my mind anyway* — and, I think, for the most part, on the page, too. But after reading and re-reading the text during editing, and after watching permaculture videos by Sean Dembrosky (Edible Acres) and grafting videos by Akiva Silver (Twisted Tree Farm), I decided to give Basil a best friend — a chosen brother. I love the name Akiva — apparently meaning *protector*, *shelter* — so I felt that was the perfect fit, and not only that, but it enriched the story, in my opinion. In the previous version, it felt like Basil's friends bailed on him and left him all alone (except for his family). After I wrote in Akiva, I felt he represented very well that part of Basil's friendliness with other people and being a part of the community.

I looked up and sent images of several women to give Benja a better idea of what I had in mind for the three ladies. These were the main muses: Julie Delpy, Kate Winslet, Amy Adams, Jennifer Connelly, Eva Mendes, Tori Amos, Geena Davis, Juliette Binoche. The public photographs I was able to find from various ceremonies and movies were extremely helpful because they provided us with visual depictions of dresses, jewellery, and body movements and angles. I am sure Benja used many other sources to help him bring this story, and the beings in it, to life on the page.

He used the following Arteza colours (and some other ones):

Lemon Yellow, hints of Sunflower Yellow, and Lilac (for her purple bits) for YELLOW FLAME, Spring Green, Mint Green and hints of Emerald Green for the clover (GREEN), Periwinkle Blue and a hint of Peacock Blue for the cornflower (BLUE), Pumpkin Orange and Orange for the pumpkin (ORANGE), Lavender for VIOLET, Indigo for INDIGO, Rose Red for RED.

As previously stated, there is a lot that goes on behind the writing, editing, illustrating, and publishing of a book. Many things that to the reader might not be evident on the surface level at first, are sensed quite a bit on the inside and can have an impact on someone years after. Details — even omitted ones, that didn't make it into the finished book — form, grow, and give a story life. It's like building soil — one may not know all the things that went into making it, but one can perceive and benefit from the richness of pieces that went in, especially when harvest time comes.

I believe the idea of writing and publishing a book with partial black and white illustrations came after I discovered *Blueberries for Sal* by Robert McCloskey, but I'm sure that wasn't the only source of inspiration. I was inclined to believe that full colour children's books are more enticing (and I still believe that), but after reading reviews and watching videos about that book, I came to the conclusion that even if the illustrations were not in full colour, the book was still very much cherished. So it gave me confidence that I could try that sort of thing with one of my stories. Some think that the illustrations in a children's book are more important than the writing (or the other way around). I think they are equally important (especially in a book such as this). *A lot of work goes into both.* I was worried that if the illustrations weren't colourful, as most of the children's books on the market are, that might cause issues with readers. When I discovered *Blueberries for Sal* and found out how loved the book was, that was proof that not every book has to have colourful illustrations. As long as they are engaging and beautifully crafted, they should be able to balance the written story well enough and together do a good job at presenting the full story in a mesmerizing way.

Books such as *Library Lion*, written by Michelle Knudsen and illustrated by Kevin Hawkes, *The Empty Pot,* by DEMI, *Rumple Buttercup,* by Matthew Gray Gubler, and *To Dance with the White Dog*, by Terry Kay, have inspired me in other wonderful ways, too, even though I wasn't clearly aware of that when writing this story. I was just writing and channelling the energy they gave me months and years ago, after being exposed to their intricate and lovely stories. *The Conversation*, by Akiva Silver, was also deeply influential.

In a time ambushed by horrible news, I wanted to write something funny, gentle, and uplifting. I also had a request to write a story about colours, something that was suggested before, but which I initially sort of dismissed after trying to write something and not being really excited by the idea or what I wrote. This time, however, after writing a few bits and pieces, and some brief dialogue lines — *which are present early in the story and remained unchanged through all the editing rounds* — I felt a story unfolding and I noticed I was giggling out loud. I took that as a good sign, so I kept on writing, and here we are. It was also important I received confirmation about certain things. I specifically remember walking with my partner on a pathway back from a park — *I think it was a sunny day, but hey, it could have been windy and drizzling with rain, too, it has been a while since then* — and discussing the story. I was listening to his remarks to get a sense if he liked the story or not. After all, he asked for it. Among other things, he mentioned he was pleasantly surprised by the apparition of the baby dragons, them being given colour names by Basil, and how it all came together at the end. He seemed excited by the story and that gave me more joy and confidence for investing more time, effort, and money to make a real book out of it. I shared the story with Benja as well and when he confirmed liking it, too, my excitement grew further. Earlier on in the year, I had been considering and planning to have illustrated, and then published, two shorter stories I had previously written. After writing this one, I felt it was the story I wanted to make next because I thought it will have greater potential to make more of us joyous and help me make a living with my writing.

Basil's evolution

In 2010 I had an exhibition in Canterbury, Kent, United Kingdom, representing my father's sculptures. One of the woodcarvings was of Saint Basil. I remember I thought it was a somewhat funny name, once translated from Romanian to English. It's different than Vasile, which is the actual Romanian name for the saint. Vasile was the name of my partner's father, and his, too, actually. Basil is also a beautiful plant, both for cooking, and for having in one's garden. I like putting it on pizza and in sandwiches. That's the meaning of the word *basil* I've been most exposed and used to. I named the protagonist 'Basil' because of all these reasons, in case you're wondering about the thought process behind someone's name in a story.

I also named him 'Sean' and was planning to use it for the cover and the title, too, but several beta readers mentioned that 'Sean Basil and the Waltz of Colours' was quite long, and one raised the issue of 'Sean' being a common Irish name. I didn't want to pinpoint where *my Basil* was from because I wanted readers to imagine themselves in his shoes with ease. I like the meaning of the name a lot, however, which, according to some websites, seems to be *God is gracious*, and because I initially gave it to the protagonist after a real inspiring person (Sean Dembrosky), I decided to still keep it in the story in the first few instances we learn about Basil, but not on the cover or in the title of the book.

I wanted Basil to be perceived as a calm, tender, and capable protector, so I researched a few photos of martial art masters. I looked at sketches and photos with Bruce Lee and others I could find, particularly for the scene in which Basil is protecting the baby dragons. When I was younger, myself and other children used to watch over our animals feeding on the hills so they wouldn't get lost, hurt, and/or eaten by wild creatures such as brown bears. My older cousin would tell us stories about Bruce Lee (and his son Brandon) and we would practice moves we saw him pictured doing in magazines or in movies. It was something fun and also educational to do while passing the time. That's what children from my generation used to do back then when people didn't have easy access to internet and modern devices — we would go exploring in the woods, climbing cherry trees, and playing all sorts of games outdoors. I'm not surprised at all that something from those times remained deeply encased in my mind and ended up in this story (and probably in others to come).

Putting the finishing touches to the illustrations was strange and quite terrifying, for both Benja and me. The illustrations are hand-drawn — *old-style, not digitally* — so any little brush stroke in the wrong direction or thickness could have jeopardized them.

Once those details were sorted, I waited for the illustrations to be delivered by post. Then, once I had them, I photographed (in front of a window, which allowed plenty of natural light in, on a cloudy day, so the light wasn't too harsh for the images), edited, and added them to the book's layout, as planned in advance.

Don't think you need fancy or expensive tools to achieve your goals. Although those things can be helpful, they are not essential. For example, I wrote, edited, and designed this book on an old, slow laptop (bought in 2011/2012, I think).

I used the Evernote app to make notes on my phone and write scenes while in bed, when I was not at my laptop, many times after midnight, sometimes even until five or six o'clock in the morning. I also used paper and pencil to make brief notes. Those can be extremely useful to have, especially if there's a power cut, which was never the case for this book, but I think it's worth mentioning — it's better to be prepared than not have the necessary tools.

In the past, I used Scrivener, Evernote, and canva.com to write, organize, and design longer and shorter books, but I learned and used Affinity Publisher to design this one.

On my YouTube channel (*Crina-Ludmila Cristea Independent Author*) and my Instagram *(lilybloomwriter)* you can find out more details about this book, my previous and upcoming ones, and the life of an indie author, in general. Some photography, gardening, and cooking videos are also available there, mostly for enjoyment and relaxation purposes. I am by no means an expert in those fields, although I have taught myself various skills by practice and by taking and completing several courses. There are always things to be learnt, in many different ways. This book is a source of education. I hope you're enjoying it, and I congratulate you on taking a step towards teaching yourself and enriching your life.

Illustrator's Note

Over the course of seven months working on this project, my personal life changed a lot. I began putting ideas to paper back in April whilst living in my flat in Canterbury. I would take my sketches to a field and design the characters amidst freshly emerging flowers and insects.

I moved out in the summer, living mostly out of my car and camping around Devon, carrying my sketchbook wherever I pitched my tent. By August I was living in a garden shed, drawing each day under the sun, whose light was almost blinding as it bounced off the white papers.

October brought a chill to shed life, so I moved into my partner's home in Peterborough. By now, daylight was short, and often I would be squinting in the dark to see what details I was adding to the nearly finished drawings. In November, the illustrations were complete.

Throughout these changes in season and lifestyle, the drawings remained a consistent part of my daily life — like anchors. Reaching the end of this project was a relief and a joy to see everything finished, but with it came a sense of loss as I realized just how stabilizing the process had been. But now that they are out of my hands and have come into yours, I am happy and hope that you enjoy them as much as I enjoyed making them.

Early

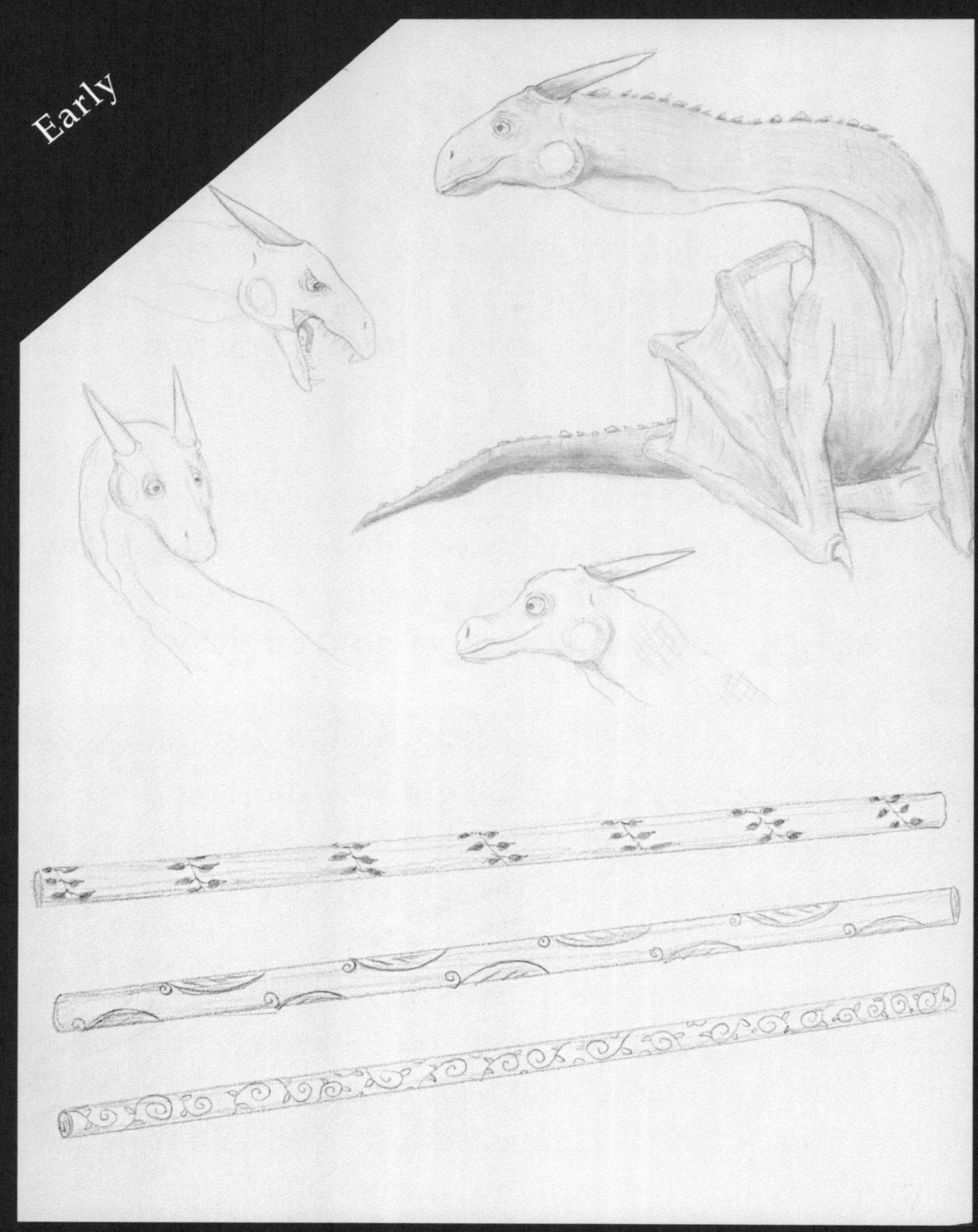

sketches of the dragon, the stick,

Basil,

the baby dragons, and the three ladies

ACKNOWLEDGEMENTS

I wholeheartedly thank the following people:

Vasile-Florin Vîlsan, for bugging me to write a story about a world without colour; this wouldn't exist otherwise, and it may be my favourite piece I have written so far. I'm sure what came out of my mind is different than what you envisioned in yours, and I'm glad to know you like the result. Thank you also for challenging me and for being patient and supportive. Here's to our forest.

Sean Dembrosky (and Sasha) from Edible Acres, for the delightful videos and warmth you communicate with, and Akiva Silver from Twisted Tree Farm, for writing and publishing Trees of Power *and especially* The Conversation *which provided me with the answer to the question, "What is your favourite book?" Without the wonderful inspiration and knowledge you give, this book wouldn't be the way it is. My 'soil' — our community's soil — is doing much better thanks to your work and way of being.*

Flock Finger Lakes, for the cool video interviews. My Therapy Garden, too.

Benja Hughes, for the vibrant, flamboyant, and thoughtful images which once again filled me with joy. I'm so grateful you stopped and allowed me to photograph you on the street that day.

Violeta Andronache, Judith Thomson, Felix and Faye, Kamba Abudu, for providing feedback at various stages in the making of this book.

Ramona, Alex, Nico, Martin, Elena, and Loredana, for encouragement.

BuyMeACoffee supporters (JD Estrada, Lucica Pătrulescu, Brian Bothwell, Paul Jones, Elisa Gallegos, Elena Hristova Patel, John Sarzoza Jr, Stacie Kay Randall, Steven Webb, Kamba Abudu, Mike Crouch, Emma Rosen), for your generous and thoughtful 'coffees' which surprised me every time, and enabled me to take another big step on this indie publishing path.

Jonathan Drori, for the massive support gifted to this project. It came at the right time, when it was needed the most. And for the great inspiration and knowledge about trees and plants you, too, share with the world.

My grandpa Ștefan, my grandpa Ion (Nicu), my grandma Marița (Maricica), and my grandma Sanda (Stanca). My father (Florin) and my mother (Maria). My aunt Carmen, the little humans (who are not so little anymore) — Ștefan, Anca, David, Andru, Denisa, Serena, Radu, Nicole — and the rest of my extended family. This story wouldn't be what it is without you in my life.

Octavian Munteanu, for writing stories and briefly sharing them with me when we were young; it was the first proper glimpse I had at a living writer and storyteller, and that, too, inspired me to think I could write a book that will make someone's day brighter.

You, dear explorer, for purchasing this story and maybe others before. Your support means a lot. I hope that my writing brings you inspiration and joy, and that you'll spread the word about it with others.

Last, but not least, to the Great Creator.

Thank you all.

— Crina-Ludmila Cristea

The process of illustrating a book can often be a very long and lonely one; involving long hours of staring at paper while the sun shines outside, drinking mug after mug of coffee, day after day.

For this reason I want to thank everyone who has been so patient with me during this project, for allowing my mind to wander off into a world of dragons and giant moons, for listening to me when I puzzled over the placement of pumpkins, and for helping me choose the all-important colours for near-microscopic pairs of shoes worn by villagers on distant hilltops.

Massive thanks to my girlfriend Leaf, who fulfilled all of the aforementioned roles on many, many occasions; and to her family, who have helped me through the end stages of the project and provided me with endless support every day (often in the form of coffees and plentiful food).

Thanks, Mum, for allowing me to step out of the tent and live in the shed while the sun was too hot and the rain was too heavy, and, again, for reminding me that eating real-life food is just as important as drawing!

And thank you to the author, creator of all of this, Crina. Thank you for entrusting me with your vision for a second time, and for allowing me to draw myself into your wonderful world of storytelling. And thank you for stopping me that day in the street to take my picture, all those years ago.

— Benja Hughes

A SMALL COLOURING COLLECTION OF FANTASTICAL WOODLAND FLORA AND FAUNA

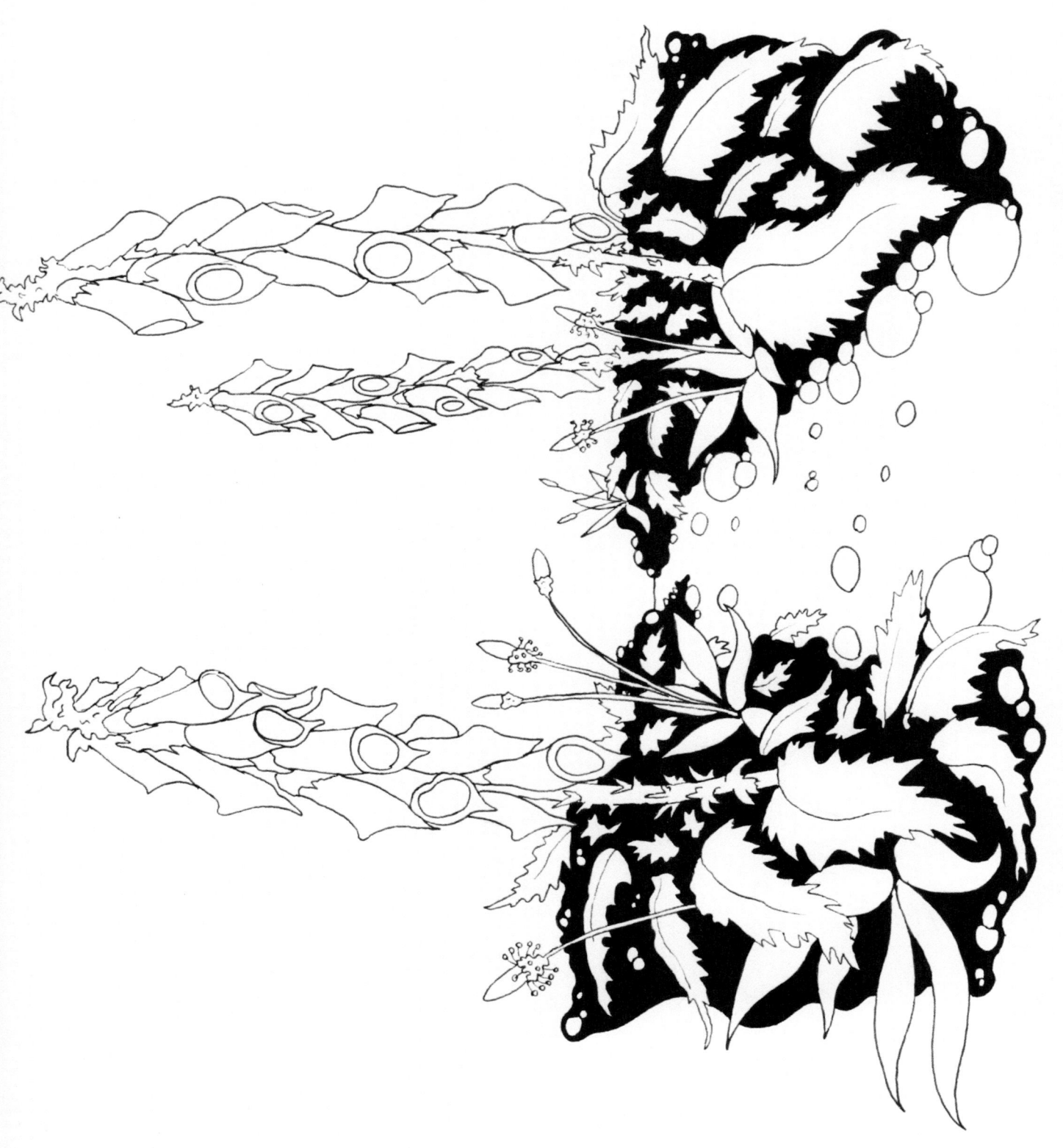

WRITE YOUR STORY

Write a story about...

... a time spent in the forest.

It can be about something that happened or a total invention of your imagination. You can mix fact and fiction, too.

Don't worry about making mistakes. You can cross words out and write others instead. In fact, I encourage you to write your story, leave it for a few weeks, and then come back to it and see if anything needs editing or rewriting.

*Please don't let yourself be restrained by the word 'forest'. You can write about whatever (place, being, and experience) you want. It is *your* story.

In order to entice your readers, try to answer the questions on the following page, and give as many details as you feel appropriate and necessary to make your story come alive and be as believable as possible.

If you are overwhelmed by the myriad of possibilities, write a few 'connector' words first. Pick the ones that stir your imagination the most and make you excited to write about.

For example, here are some of mine:

naughty chestnut, the whispering tree, frozen lake, reverie, gigantic water lilies, candy cane, petals, glowing mushrooms, fireflies, snow, river of dreams, the haunted cabin, quince, etc.

Who were you with?

What flora and fauna have you found, discovered and identified?

What did you eat and how did you cook your meal?

Have you built a shelter out of branches, sticks, and leaves, or brought one with you in the form of a tent?

Did you encounter any dangers? How did you overcome them?

How was the weather? Was it sunny, were the leaves turning golden and rusty, falling in the gentle wind, making a pleasant carpet underneath your feet, or did you have to find a shelter to keep safe from the storm?

What about the beings you met on your stay and during your voyage and adventure through the forest?

What did you like the most about your time in the forest: the colours of the leaves, the textures of a certain tree bark, the taste of wild cherries, the perfume of ripe blueberries, the wind whistling through the lime-green leaves, or something else entirely?

Did you carry a notebook and a pencil to write your thoughts and observations in, like Basil did? Did you capture any photographs or videos? Did you make audio recordings?

What did the forest and your exploration teach you so far?

Add/use photographs and sketches to help bring your story to life*

What would you like to discover next?

Author's End Note

For as long as I can remember, I felt stories are the key to people's hearts. Stories connect individuals, and groups of people, whether we want that or not. Stories have great power. They can change lives. They have saved mine many times. They have been a key to my happiness and well-being, even/especially when the stories I was reading made me cry, which occurred several times. That didn't deter me from reading, in fact, it fueled my hunger and filled me with wonder — it made me want to read and write more than ever.

Books are about taking chances. You never know exactly how a story is going to be when you start reading (or when the story is being read to you), unless, of course, you've read or heard it before. There is always a risk to be frustrated or bored, but there is also a tremendous, much greater, opportunity for gaining education and entertainment. Beware of books, they can break your heart. They can also mend it and fill it with joy. They expand our world by offering different points of view and emotions which we wouldn't be able to have access to otherwise.

One of the most incredible things stories bring to us is that they manage to make an invisible bond between strangers — both dead and alive — on different continents, in peculiar times, when we least expect it. When we most need it. That is the beauty of storytelling — one of many.

This story, too, has been a connector, so far between a couple of us, and I hope it will continue to be one among many individuals in the years to come. If there is something I would like to leave behind as my legacy, whenever the time will come, it's this:

a welcome bond between beings — to respect, love, and cherish. I don't know if I'll achieve that. I can only hope and have faith my actions will reach that goal in time, at least for a couple of individuals. Everything else regarding this is a mystery to me.

If all this sounds a bit strange, or too intense, hey, stories can make the heart pump faster, cause a bed to shake from someone's snoring, or change entire societies. Yes, I have witnessed that. Beware of stories. They can make you live in other worlds, they can propel you to think, feel, and care.

Best wishes,
Crina.

ABOUT THE ARTISTS

Crina-Ludmila Cristea is an independent author. She is passionate about permaculture and food forest designs. Originally from Vrancea, Romania, she currently lives in the UK.

Benja Hughes is an illustrator, musician, and multidisciplinary artist. He draws inspiration from the natural world in each of his creative endeavours. Benja is also a passionate wildlife photographer, originally from Exeter, UK.

Printed in Poland
by Amazon Fulfillment
Poland Sp. z o.o., Wrocław
27 July 2022

c1222a18-e02a-435a-a92c-687b2b6b5342R02